The Paradise Chronicles

Rufus Yates

The Paradise Chronicles
Copyright © 2020 by Rufus Yates

Library of Congress Control Number: 2020906911
ISBN-13: Paperback: 978-1-64749-105-5
          Hardcover: 978-1-64749-107-9
          ePub: 978-1-64749-106-2

All rights reserved. No part of this publication may be reproduced, distributed, or transmitted in any form or by any means, including photocopying, recording, or other electronic or mechanical methods, without the prior written permission of the publisher or author, except in the case of brief quotations embodied in critical reviews and certain other noncommercial uses permitted by copyright law.

Although every precaution has been taken to verify the accuracy of the information contained herein, the author and publisher assume no responsibility for any errors or omissions.No liability is assumed for damages that may result from the use of information contained within.

Printed in the United States of America

GoToPublish LLC
1-888-337-1724
www.gotopublish.com
info@gotopublish.com

The year is 2025, the age of Nanotechnology, artificial intelligence, and the race for nuclear supremacy, a time of prosperity for many and a time of violence and war for others. As threats of a nuclear war points its bloody finger at the eastern shores of the United States, some concerned citizens living in the east choose to move westward, seeking safety from the nuclear fallout that would surely follow.

My family and I recently relocated to Three Crossing, California (a small town in the foothills of Redwood Valley). We had to make a choice: either remain in Bristol, Virginia and keep the same job or relocate to California and get three times the salary. Bristol is a small friendly town on the Tennessee border and the only town in the United States with a main street divided by two states. I was offered a once in a lifetime opportunity with the company I work for and moving to California was part of the deal. Relocating was heartbreaking and life-changing as it meant leaving our home as well as our family and friends in Bristol and starting a new life in California.

My wife and I were both born and raised in Bristol. We have two kids in a local school, and one that's old enough to start pre-school, asking them to pack-up and leave their friends and move thousands of miles away was one of the hardest things I've ever had to do. We sat down with the kids and discussed what it would mean having thrice the income to live on, not to mention all the opportunities of well-paying jobs available for them after

high school, if they choose not to go to college (which is paid by the company).

We all agreed; the opportunities for us in California far outweighed the ones in Bristol. I told them that to prosper in this world, we all must make sacrifices.

My promotion would consist of a brand new five-bedroom house on a secluded, eighteen- acre lot with an in-ground pool just outside of Lake Town, California. Along with the pay increase, I would get a brand-new Chevy Suburban and a whole list of other incentives.

Laura and I had discussed moving to the west on several occasions over the years but we neither had the finances nor the job security that is being offered to us now. We would most likely never get another opportunity like this one.

Our kids would receive full college scholarships including free housing, along with a personal savings bond redeemable at age eighteen, plus all the other benefits. The job opportunities for Michael and Megan are, without a doubt, ten times more profitable in California compared to Bristol.

The latest sanctions placed on Iran only increased the tensions between our countries. The threat of a nuclear missile aimed at Washington, D.C. helped us make our decision to move out west. Living in Bristol, only a few hundred miles from the number one target area in the country for a nuclear attack, would have greatly reduced our odds of surviving, and California being thousands of miles from ground zero should give us better odds.

My name is Jim Osgood. I'm a program developer for A.I.M.E. Industries. We specialize in Artificially Intelligent Medical Equipment for hospitals (robot surgeons you might say), our robots assist doctors in life-saving operations, greatly increasing

the chances for a successful outcome. Robots don't make mistakes, only the person using it may.

My wife, Laura, put on hold her teaching career to raise our youngest daughter, Jamie, who is now five and will be starting school next year. Our son, Michael, is a senior this year and our oldest daughter, Megan, is a sophomore. We now live in California, where we're slowly adjusting to the change of atmosphere with great enthusiasm.

The hardest part of our move was breaking the news to my parents, that we were taking their grandchildren three thousand miles away to the other side of the country to live, and that we only had two weeks before we had to leave. Our kids grew up around my mom and dad as well as my brother's children, and they saw each other every week and are really close to each other.

I made a promise to Mom and Dad to bring the kids at least twice a year to see them, and of course, we have Skype which would help us keep in touch. I tried to get Mom and Dad to move with us; we have plenty of room in our new house, and the kids begged them to come too but like I said before, it's hard to leave the only home you've ever known and I couldn't pry Dad out of Bristol with a bull-dozer.

Laura's mom and dad moved to Florida a few years ago to spend their golden years in the warm sunshine, they have a really nice place in Hollywood, Florida and they were glad to see us move to California.

My brother, Steve, and his wife, Linda, have two kids who are like brother and sister to my kids. They will help keep Mom and Dad company while we're away. Still, it wouldn't be the same. It's not easy to leave your home and loved ones but the opportunities for us in California would make it impossible to pass up.

The fight in Iran never seems to stop, the pressure keeps building more and more each day and I fear the lid will soon blow off like an old unpredictable pressure cooker that my grandmother might have used. That is one of the advantages of our move to the west; we'll be thousands of miles away from Washington, D.C., which would give us some chance to survive a missile attack at least.

We decided to take our time on the trip to California; we tried to make it a vacation, and I think we all enjoyed having the time together. Life tends to get in the way of living, as the days go by, families can grow apart very easily. If you don't make the time to be together, you might wake up one morning wondering where everyone went. It seems like in the blink of an eye, my son has gone from being a toddler to a teenager, and the memories we shared in those seventeen years seem to be few and somewhat incomplete, at least in my memory bank. It's as though I was gone for a long time only to return to find a young man where the boy once was.

There's a lot to see while traveling across this big beautiful country and Tennessee, the first state on our road-trip-list, has more interesting tourist attractions and famous sites to enjoy than any other state on our route. You don't have to plan your stops; all you need to do is simply take the time to stop and smell the roses when you see the signs. There are numerous dinosaur land attractions and natural caves, as well as the famous towns and music halls—not to mention all the great places to eat and so many other things to see and do, much more than we had time for.

Kids grow up so fast. Now, in this age of technological wonders, we are so busy trying to make enough money to pay the bills and put food on the table and clothes on our backs that we don't have time for each other. We need to take advantage of every moment we have with each other. Make the time to go to our kid's school events and get to know their friends and their parents; find out what they like to do and join them in their adventures; be their friend while they're still young.

Michael was able to take advantage of our never-ending road trip to get some quality driving experience. I tried to let him take the wheel every chance I could. Laura and I sat in the back with the girls while he chauffeured us around. I could see a change in his confidence and I noticed his heightened concentration while driving. By the end of our trip, I could trust him with the new Suburban without watching his every move.

Laura and I even made the time for a long-overdue honeymoon, one that we had sacrificed to our jobs some years ago. While we were in Los Angeles, we decided to take advantage of the opportunity, while Laura and I were having a night on the town, the kids found plenty of things to occupy themselves. There is no lack of things to do in L.A.

The western sunset in L.A. was magical, even more beautiful than the pictures we had seen in so many movies and magazines. Laura and I really enjoyed our mini-honeymoon, it had been long overdue.

I must admit, with all the road-time this past week and the attractions it was nice to be on our way to our new home. We still had a long way to go to get to Redwood Valley which is located some fifty-plus miles east of Fort Bragg. I thought Tennessee was a long state until we left from Los Angeles (LA) to go to Redwood Valley, we must have gone over a thousand miles since leaving LA; thank God for GPS is all I can say. The country we saw on the way to northern California was beautiful; it made the long road trip worthwhile.

Our new home is even nicer than I expected it to be. We're far enough away from the city yet close enough to the hospitals and schools. The house is enormous; there's plenty of room for Mom and Dad to stay and Laura loves the large open kitchen.

The garage is big enough to hold four cars but part of it will be my shop, there's plenty of property to ride ATV's and have some horses if we like.

The school's transfer papers and medical records for the kids were taken care of before we left Bristol. All they had to do was show up and start making new friends.

Mike and Megan both seemed to be happy with their new school, even though I could tell, they missed their friends back home. Mike is a senior and only had six months of school left before graduating, and Megan is a sophomore and has so many close friends she left behind in Bristol. I know it's hard for her, but it seems like the new kids at school always get plenty of attention, and that's just fine with Megan. The more the merrier. Mike, on the other hand, is a little more reserved, almost to the point of being shy. On the first day of school, Megan brought two friends home with her, they seemed to be nice girls (I think they were more interested in Michael than they were in Megan).

Most of the accents in this area are a lot like ours, except they use fewer words than we do. The temperatures here so far have been wonderful. We all like the warm weather. Everyone we have met seem to be very friendly and welcoming.

Our nearest neighbors are Sid and Mary Phipps, they have a daughter, Lisa, who is sixteen years old and is quite mature for her age. She's already taken up with Megan, and she's obviously interested in Michael.

Sid is a tall, slender, friendly fellow, sort of a professor-type guy. He's an engineer and a good inventor. I would describe him as a perfectionist. Sid's backyard is covered with mechanical metal sculptures, made from parts and pieces of junkyard metal scraps most of which are discarded car parts and tractor implements. I think the kids call it 'steam-punk art'. I really like his dragon sculpture; the majestic creature is so perfectly represented with gears and cogs of every description. The figures have obviously taken years of his time to build.

Sid's wife Mary is a grown-up version of her daughter Lisa, bubbly, and friendly and quite attractive. Mary is also a teacher at the elementary school where our youngest daughter Jamie attends school.

One of the most popular pastimes here in Northern California is prepping, which is simply preparing for a global disaster, or the end of time, or any other life-threatening event that may arise. In being prepared, one must look ahead to the future in order to make life as easy as possible if a disaster occurs.

Sid is determined to be the best prepper ever, and he's got his heart set on teaching me the system too. I have to say he's a good teacher; he explains everything in a simple, easy-to-understand method.

In this part of the country, there's an abundance of caves in the nearby mountains, some of the preppers have been buying up tracts of land that have caves on them to use for private fallout shelters, and now, I'm the proud owner of a cave next door to Sid's. Our caves are close enough together for an adjoining doorway (like adjoining rooms at a motel). Sid estimates there is about three feet of dirt left to remove between our cave and his, at the point he has marked. I'll take his word for it since I know very little about surveying, but I trust Sid, he's a pretty smart guy.

Sid's been working on his safe house for over five years. He sold me the extra cave he had bought just in case some of his family or friends needed a bunker. I feel privileged since he had chosen me and my family to save from the apocalypse.

Sid has transformed what was a hole in the side of a mountain to very comfortable living quarters. He's built walls, ran electric wires throughout the cave and made the place look just like a house on the inside. He's stocked everything you need to survive in the event of a major disaster from electrical power through solar panels, wind turbines and a diesel generator for backup, to running water and satellite TV. He has plenty of food and water to last for months, also cold storage and even a waste disposal system. He even installed a gas toilet that I am yet to see. Sid has everything planned out and is waiting for the opportunity to put it all to use.

Lately, we've been working on our (Osgood's) cave and I'm proud of how it's coming along. Sid will make sure we have everything we need to survive when the time comes, and that gives me some peace of mind.

Laura is yet to see our mountain hideaway, but today she'll get her chance to approve or disapprove of all the hard work we've done; she's often described our prepping as overactive paranoia. I've tried to convince her of just how close we are to this Iranian conflict becoming a real disaster; every night as we watch the latest news, I can hear the fear in the reporter's voice because he knows his job is very dangerous, and his news agency may need a replacement for him at any time, though his wife and three children will have no substitute.

To my surprise, Laura actually liked the cave. She approved of the work we had done. She said it just needed some curtains and a lot of paint. I told her whatever she wanted was fine with me, we'll paint it pink if she wanted.

Mom called us last night to make sure we were keeping up with the news. She was worried after watching the latest reports on the Iran conflict. Mom usually doesn't get so upset over the news, but I could tell it was really bothering her now. The peace talks that have been going on for at least two years now don't seem to be going too well. There for a while, we thought things would work out but now, we're even closer than ever to another war. The Iranian's threats of launching missiles at Washington, D.C. are being taken very seriously. Many people in the D.C. area have been leaving until things de-escalate.

How some religions can be so cruel to their own people and feel that they're doing what their god wants them to, is beyond me. A woman has no rights in Iran and they're treated like slaves–living only to serve the men that control their every move–and to raise their children to hate everyone that doesn't believe the same way.

Tomorrow evening, Mike and I plan to take some supplies to the cave, just a few odds and ends that we've been walking around for the past few weeks in the garage, fuel tanks for the gas stove, some fresh batteries for flashlights, and electrical equipments: a radio and a police-scanner which should come in handy, along with some dried food that is supposed to last for years, and sleeping bags for the kids that we keep forgetting to bring. We've been using our cave as a storage shed here lately just to keep the garage from getting over-run.

While we were busy unloading our supplies, Sid and Mary showed up with their daughter Lisa. They had a large load of groceries that they were carrying to the cave and I could see something had Sid upset. He gets this intense frown that makes his eyes look closed when he's stressed out about something, and right now he could use a seeing eye dog.

The fresh vegetables they brought along wouldn't last very long in the cave unless they were going to stay there and eat them now. I walked over to help him carry some of his things to his cave after we finished unloading our stuff and he said that they were going to spend the weekend in the cave.

"Really? Maybe we'll stay one night next weekend. I guess it is a good idea to practice," I said.

"You didn't watch the news today, did you, Jim?" he asked.

"No, I haven't had a chance. What's going on?" I asked.

"I'm afraid Iran is getting ready to follow through with their threats any time now," he said in a low voice trying not to scare the kids.

"I didn't even turn the radio on today," I replied.

"Come on, grab one of those boxes and help me unload, I'll fill you in on the latest," he said.

While Sid filled me in on the latest bad news on the conflict with Iran that we have all been dreading, he begged me to get Laura and the kids and stay in the cave tonight. I could tell by the look in his eyes (that were barely visible), that he was dead serious. I would have to go home to get Laura and the girls and the roads are probably packed by now. I don't want Laura to drive in heavy traffic; she's still not used to this area yet.

I called Laura and told her to pack everything we needed for a couple of days and that I would be there as soon as I could. There was no way I could tell her what was happening without scaring her half to death, so I just told her straight out: we will have to stay in the cave tonight and that Sid believes Iran is going to launch a missile any time now. She had been watching the news today and some of our family and friends had already called to warn her. She said she was getting ready to call me when I called.

Looks like everyone had heard the news but me; the roads were jam-packed. I sat in traffic for a short while then I thought this would be a good time to try out the four-wheel drive on the new Suburban. I just dropped down on the side of the road and went around all the traffic, when I looked in the rear view mirror and noticed a long line of cars following me leaving a huge cloud of dust (not for the faint of heart) in our exodus.

When I got back on the road, I called Mom and Dad to find out what was going on back in Virginia. Dad said everyone was in a panic after hearing the news reports, some people were trying to take too many things with them to the shelters. He said they were on their way to the local fallout shelter along with my brother and his family. He added that the National Guard had been going through the neighborhoods telling everyone to go to a shelter, that's something he had never seen before, not even during World War II. I told him to let Steve and his son, Jimmy, do the heavy lifting and to make sure they got all their prescription medications before they left, and try not to worry about us. you guys just be careful, we're on our way to the cave now and I'll call you later tonight.

It's a scary thing when you realize that this may be the last time you ever get to talk to your Mom and Dad and you're so far away that you can't help them, no matter how much you want to, you can't just give them a big hug and console them. I need to stop worrying about them. After all, Steve is there to help them. I've got to concentrate on protecting my family here.

The stores were full of people now—all fighting over the last few items on the shelves. We did manage to get some bacon, eggs and milk, and some fresh-store pizzas to take to the cave with us. We had plenty of canned foods and dried emergency food stocked in the cave already, we'd make do.

We passed three accidents on the way back to the cave. We got lucky as all the traffic was going north and we were going south. People were getting scared and making mistakes. Panic would have killed us as easily as a bomb would.

I told Sid what my mom and dad were going through back in Virginia as we unloaded my car. This only reassured his decision to stay in the caves tonight.

Sid and I stayed outside the caves, planning our line of defense while listening to the news on our cell phones. We had no signal on the phones inside the caves and the kids were watching movies on the TV. So we stayed out a little after dusk then decided to call it a night.

Sid suggested we should work on the thruway after we get settled in, and he would be working on the wall from his side.

As uninviting as the cave looks, I do feel somewhat safer here, I thought to myself as I closed the heavy metal door to the entrance behind me. After all, that's why we've been working so hard to get this place ready, so we would have a safe place to go at times like this. Who knows, this may be our home for a while. I just wish we had stocked more supplies when we had the chance, but that will be a lesson for me. As soon as I have the first chance to get everything we need, I'll make the cave top priority.

We've installed all the latest security systems on the entrance doors to our caves as well as made them airtight and bombproof. We also mounted trail camps around the front perimeter to deter trespassers, and to use as our windows since the caves didn't come with a window option. Our long-range antenna is over two hundred feet above the mountain. It should let us keep in touch with the outside world. We should have everything we need to keep us safe and comfortable for a while, at least for a few weeks.

"Sorry, we didn't get to give her a paint job, honey," I joked as I entered the cave.

"As long as we're safe and all together is all that really matters now," she replied.

Our phones had no signal in the cave, so I tried the CB (Citizens Band) radio which should be working, since it's wired straight to a one-hundred-foot-tall antenna, unlike the wireless phones. With all the static and mangled-up words coming from what sounded like hundreds of people all trying to talk at the same time, it was impossible to decipher the garble. There must be something interfering with the signal. The TV reception is all static too. It looks like we'll be watching a lot of DVDs. After all the checking and double-checking to get good reception in here, now it won't work. Oh well, let's have some of that pizza I smell, at least the gas range works.

"Mike, maybe we'll work on that wall in the back room after we eat, Sid assured me the spot he marked would connect our caves," I said.

I looked around for a shovel or something to dig with as I chewed on the last bite of the pizza when I remembered that that was something we hadn't brought from the garage yet- shovels and picks. I did find a three-foot long copper ground rod we had left over from running some electrical wires and a two-pound hammer. Then I began driving the rod into the thick compacted dirt of the cave wall, with considerable effort and a little sweat from swinging the hammer I managed to drive a couple feet of the rod into the hard soil. I could hear a pinging sound, it was coming from the rod. Evidently, Sid was banging on the rod from the other side. We signaled each other in a crude Morse code that neither of us could understand, then we resumed our excavation project. Sid assured me the dirt was only two or three feet thick at this point and he was right on the money.

While I was struggling to remove the ground rod from the cave wall, Michael said he felt a breeze coming from the wall and asked me what I thought it was. Sure enough, there was a continuous flow of air coming out of the wall as if it were the wind from the outside of the cave but this was coming from inside of the mountain. I got my meter to check the air quality and the needle didn't move at all, that meant the air was originating from somewhere inside the mountain and hadn't been contaminated. This would supply a constant flow of fresh air for our caves eliminating the need for the bottles of oxygen we had stocked earlier. After a few more minutes of chiseling on the wall, the air poured through the opening like a stream of water. "You must have found a cavern," I told Michael.

"Dad you're not going to believe this but, now I think I hear water running," he said.

I put my ear to the opening and sure enough, I could hear what sounded like a stream of running water.

"I think you're right, son. There must be a stream on the other side of this wall, and if it's clean water, we may need it to drink," I said.

"I'll get a light so we can see what's in there," Mike said.

"Son, don't make that hole too big, we don't have anything to cover it up with. That may be a cavern, and there could be something living in there and we don't want any bears or zombies visiting us in the night, do we?"

We got a good light and shined it in the golf ball size opening that Mike had gouged in the cave wall and sure enough there was a large cavity on the other side as well as a stream.

"Let's leave this wall until tomorrow, son. Like I said, we don't know what we might find on the other side. Just find something to block that hole off with for tonight."

I finally managed to wrestle the copper ground rod back out of the wall (connecting our two caves) leaving a penny-size hole to try and communicate through. I could see a light coming from the other side of the hole and noticed something moving around.

"Hello, is anybody in there?" I shouted into the small opening with my hands cupped around my mouth.

"No! There's no one home, just keep digging," was the muffled reply from the tiny hole. We continued with our excavation and in a little over thirty minutes, Sid and I were shaking hands through the now-enlarged opening in the wall, and after another thirty minutes, Sid and I were enjoying a nice hot cup of coffee together sitting at my kitchen table.

Sid was really excited about the cavern that Michael had accidentally discovered while digging the thruway. He said his charts had indicated some streams behind the cave wall, but they couldn't say exactly where.

Mike was busy working to enlarge the opening between our caves so Mary and Lisa could join us, while Sid and I were trying to figure out why we had no radio or TV reception. We knew it would take a major black-out to stop our reliable CB radios from working. The radio towers would have to be offline everywhere somehow, or our coax would have to be disconnected or cut into, and that doesn't sound very likely given we had just checked them.

We had some hot pizza and a good long talk. The seriousness of our situation seemed to disappear in the conversation as we discussed our plan of action before giving in, and calling it a night. Sid and Mary went to their safe house while their daughter, Lisa, stayed with us for the night. The kids stayed up late watching zombie movies of all things.

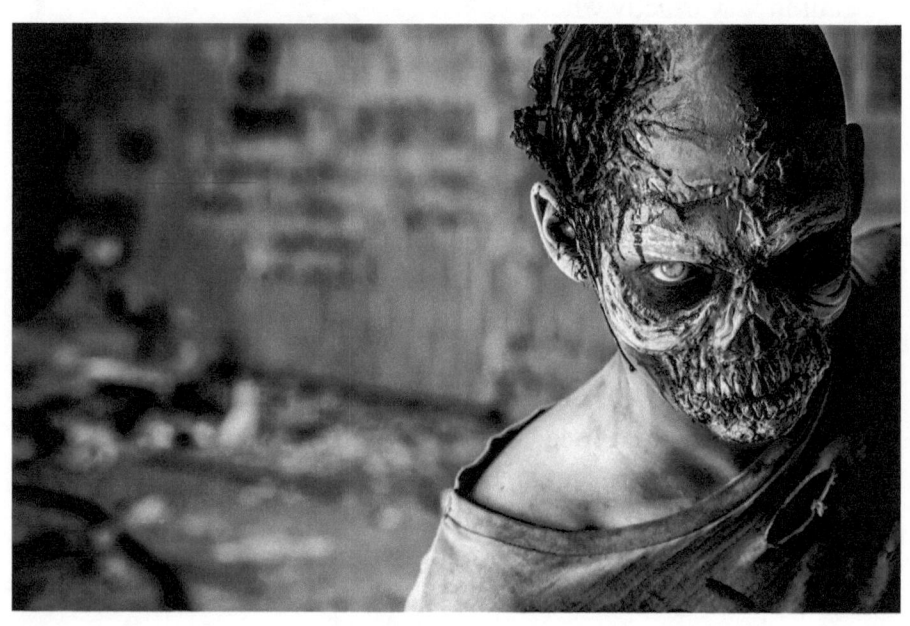

The children's laughter was a welcomed sound after all the confusion of the day. It felt good to just lie down. Our new bed was worth every dime we gave for it, all the stress and aches and pains seemed to melt away as I lay there trying to adjust my mind to the reality of the events that we had witnessed this day. I slept like a baby. I doubt if a bear could have woke me up. Laura said she never slept a wink. She tossed and turned all night worrying about bears coming through the walls. Where she got that idea… I really don't know.

I love the smell of bacon; I don't care where I am, it always makes me smile. I was awakened to that smell every day growing up back home. Virginia is a big ham and bacon producer for the country, and my parents and grandparents never shied away from any kind of pork. Laura and Mary were busy trying to make our first breakfast in the cave a memorable one while Sid and I checked the air quality inside and out, and the readings hadn't changed since yesterday.

"Enjoy the bacon everybody, because that's all we could get in such short notice, we didn't get to stock up on fresh meats and vegetables as we planned. The stores were already sold out of everything before we could get there."

"Don't worry honey we've got two nice Virginia hams hanging in the back of the cave we can eat," I said.

After breakfast, we continued working on the mystery cavern, with three of us digging it wasn't long before we were entering the newly discovered cavern.

"Mike, get our head-strap-lights. I'll get my pistol. You never know what we might find in there," I told him.

The sound of running water was amplified in the dark cavern, along with the pounding of our heartbeats. A small stream—

about three feet wide—was running through the middle of the cavern leaving ample room to walk on either side.

"We should test this water, it may be better than what we've been drinking," Sid noted.

As we continued deeper into the dark cavern, I thought of the coal miners back in southwest Virginia as well as Kentucky and West Virginia working underground for eight or ten hours a day. Some of the mines are only twenty-eight inches from top to bottom, leaving no choice for the men but to lie on their sides to perform their jobs. While receiving a decent salary to feed their families nutritious meals, a shortened life expectancy would be their final reward for a lifetime working in the black gold. Some miners would have the privilege of working in high-coal where you couldn't even touch the top but it was known to everyone to be much more dangerous than the low mines due to rocks falling and the walls giving in to the added pressure.

After a quarter of a mile or so into our exploration, the cavern suddenly revealed a large open room, the walls and ceiling were somewhat smooth and concave while the top was completely out of our reach, and the cavern bottom consisted of loose dark soil (almost like potting soil) you could scoop up handfuls of it without using any tools. The soft soil reminded me of a freshly tilled garden and I thought to myself, maybe we could grow vegetables in here, we would need a good light source of course. The area was large enough for a garden and the stream running through the middle could be used to water the plants.

Leaving the large room, that we named 'the garden room', we continued our trek into the dark catacombs of the mountain, only the frequent undisturbed-cobweb would interfere with our efforts to discover a new untouched world. From what we could tell, no one had left their footprints in the soil before us. It was like a line at the beginning of an old TV show I admired as a youth to go where no man has gone before. After another hour of exploring the dark passageway and finding no signs of danger, we turned around and headed back home.

We found no signs of life, no tracks or bones, not even a bug or a spider, which brought us to the conclusion that there had been no living creatures there before us. At least in the sections we explored, there was nothing for them to eat in the cavern; no bugs for the spiders, no spiders for the rodents, and so on. We took the samples from the stream and soil back with us so that Sid could test them in his portable lab that he just happened to have in his shelter.

On the way back from our excursion, I asked Sid for his opinion on what he thought was happening on the outside with the rest of the world. He gave no theories to be disproved, only the facts that he knew for sure that the air outside the caves is toxic and if anyone is out there breathing it, they won't last long. As to what caused the radiation levels to increase suddenly, he couldn't say for sure. All we can do is keep an eye on the Geiger counters, taking readings at least twice a day. In the meantime, we should try to get the radios working so we can get some news from the outside.

We decided to continue exploring the cavern at some later date, when we were better prepared to be gone for a few days and when we could feel more comfortable to leave our families without worrying about them.

The days turned into weeks and weeks into months, each day we would test the air without so much as an inkling of a change. We had become accustomed to our dark dungeon habitats, almost comfortable, you might say, everyday life became a routine as we carried on with our lives inside the dark mountain.

Michael turned eighteen within the confines of our cave, and we celebrated with a cake, using the last of our powdered egg-mixture while hoping that we would be outside before the next birthday comes around and we could use fresh eggs in our cakes.

I wish we could have given Michael a car as we had planned to and he could celebrate with his new friends; that we don't even know whether they survived or not, while some may be prisoners like we are, stuck in their safe-houses just waiting for the day they can go back outside.

Our lack of fresh fruits and vegetables in our diets was beginning to interfere with our daily activities. The multi-vitamins that we rely on so much are no substitute for the nutrients we get from fresh fruits and vegetables, and living in the dark cave depletes our vitamin D, that with the lack of exercise was beginning to show on us all. So we decided to try to raise a vegetable garden in the cavern (garden room). We needed the fresh vegetables, and we thought we might just get a good work out while we're at it.

Sid, being the prepper that he is, saved most of the seeds from his tomatoes and cucumbers as well as some potatoes from his last load of supplies. Now we just needed some good bright lights to hang in the room to replace the sunshine, and Sid has plenty of lights in his hardware storage room. I noticed.

I would first need to remove the alternator from my car to use as a generator. We can use Jamie's bicycle that we left in front of the cave to turn the alternator, which in turn should power the lights, thus making the vegetables grow.

We bought the best hazmat suits we could find at the time: army-issued, government approved for Operation Desert Storm. They're somewhat outdated for our modern military but they should work for short maneuvers like we will be doing, hopefully.

After struggling to put the undersized hazmat suit on, I checked my oxygen mask one last time before slowly stepping out of the cave into the toxic air for the first time in months. The suit was a little small for me but it would have to do. With each step I took, my mind raced as I tried to concentrate on my surroundings. After a long look all around trying to assess any damages, I noticed that some of the leaves were still on the trees and the grass was fairly green as well. As far as I could see, there was no damage to anything in the local area. My car was covered with a thin layer of leaves and dust from four months of just sitting outside; in the thick forest, everything seemed to be untouched. Now, to get the alternator off with the few tools I brought with me, will be a miracle.

As I opened the door of my leaf-covered Suburban, I was reminded of the wonderful relationship between this fine luxury automobile and myself. How much I love the smell of her leather interior and admire the shape of her body, her power and agility beckons me to take her for a spin. I glanced in the back seat only to discover a bag of candy bars (the little bite-size ones). This will be for a special occasion, what a welcomed surprise, I thought to myself. Little things like the taste of chocolate can mean a lot when you've been without it for so long.

As I began to loosen the bolts that held the alternator tightly to the engine, I couldn't help but notice that no birds were chirping or flying around and no squirrels barking or running from tree to tree and there was a strange eerie- silence that seemed to be spying on me as I fumbled to complete my task. I thought of the zombie movies that the kids had been watching (at least once a week now) as I looked all around once more with the generator in my hand and hurried back to the cave entrance as though I were being chased by some spooky ghost. I grabbed the bicycle as I stepped through the cave entrance and then closed the heavy metal door to the outside world behind me. Now the cave felt like my sanctuary, my safe-house, and my protector.

With Sid's engineering skills and my fabricating knowledge, within three hours, we were testing our (green) power supply. We plugged the television in, while Megan peddled the bike at a steady speed. We had enough power but hardly any reception, now we could charge our batteries, power the television and do anything else we might need electricity for.

Now all we had to do was to connect the power cord to the garden lights and the fresh vegetables would be on the way. We still didn't know if our lights will make the plants grow like the sun does, but we had to try.

Lisa and Megan were both glad to pedal the bicycle if it would mean dropping a few pounds (that had been sneaking up on them since we've been in the cave), and it would give our plants the light they need to grow too.

Michael was standing by at the garden to relay the message back to us (that the lights are working), as Lisa pedaled the bicycle at an easy running pace. We heard Mike's yell of excitement (we have lights) as the cavern lit up. We all ran to the lights coming from the garden, as the illumination revealed an underground world that amazed us all. The cavern room would give us more space to breathe in our confined quarters of the cave, and just might make our lives a little more bearable.

We all stood there in the large illuminated room and just gazed in awe as we realized just how huge the cavern was. Sid estimated the site to be just over a half-acre, coming from an engineer I would bet he's close. While the lights were no replacement for the sunshine, we had faith they would help our plants to grow.

Laura passed around the plastic bag containing the small individually wrapped delicious chocolate bars, and we all indulged in a celebration of life, of being alive to enjoy the moment.

I noticed the lights flicker on and off a couple of times which reminded me that Lisa was still peddling the bicycle to give us the lights we were enjoying, and she was probably getting tired.

"Would you go take over from Lisa, Megan before we're left in the dark?" I asked.

We went back to our subterranean living quarters and gathered all of our usable seeds, Sid had some tomatoes, cucumber, and potatoes; we only had the dried beans that we stocked earlier in the year to use for planting. After all, we had no clue we'd be planting a garden in our caves.

We had only to scratch a trench in the soil to plant the seeds, and as unpleasant as it was, our waste would be needed for fertilizer. We filled half of the open ground with the seeds we had and used the stream to water them with. Once the plants mature, we will have plenty of seeds to fill the garden.

The cave garden gave us a renewed sense of hope. Until now, I had doubts whether we would have enough food to last until it was safe to go back outside.

Sid found a length of garden-hose in his seemingly unlimited supply of miscellaneous articles and suggested we build a shower, using the stream for our water supply. I told him it was his idea so he could try it out first. The water was bitter cold, running through the dark belly of the mountain; it was like plunging your arm into a cooler of icy water trying to find the last beer on a hot summer day, too cold to stand stark-naked under for very long. We've all now learned how to take one–minute showers if not quicker. It sure does make you miss having hot running water, that's for sure.

We also made use of the excess ground around the garden. It would become a walking path for some of us. Laura and I, along with Sid and Mary, have gotten quite used to the afternoon strolls around the garden after dinner. We usually turn off all lights but have that one light to imitate the moonlight. The kids are in a lot better shape now since they began running around the garden track. Our enthusiasm has increased immensely since we started

our garden projects. Everyone is a lot more active and in a better mood, too.

Now we just have to take turns pedaling the artificial sunshine to our plants, for at least four hours per day. We can't be sure whether the plants will grow but we have to try. We don't know how long we'll have to stay here.

Sid and I take readings on the outside and the inside a couple times each day but the radiation levels are still too high for us to escape from our confines.

It has now been four weeks since we planted the seeds in our underground garden and to our delight, most of the plants are thriving. At this rate, we should have fresh tomatoes in a couple more months if the plants bear fruit at all. We will have to pollinate the plants by hand when they get their blooms since we don't have any bees down here. I think a good clean q-tip will substitute for the flying critters just fine.

Sid, Michael, and I have decided to explore the cave a little deeper tomorrow morning. This time we will take provisions to last a couple of days. We may find something we can use. Who knows, we may find something we don't want too.

Laura knows her way around guns as she was raised around them back in Bristol. Her father and uncles as well as her brothers are all hunters and gun owners. I feel very comfortable leaving Laura and Mary (who is also a gun user) to watch over the girls while we are gone. If no one opens the outer doors, they'd be fine was out primary belief.

I know everyone is getting cabin fever stuck in the cave all this time. I feel the same way; but there's not much we can do about it right now. Hopefully, we will be back outside soon.

Excited to be continuing the exploration of the cavern, I woke up early, eager to get started. We checked our gear twice and are now confident that we have everything we'll need for our trip.

We set off to find the source of the fresh air that fills the cavern. As we passed by our subterranean garden, I couldn't help but feel a sense of pride seeing all the plants growing so well and knowing our efforts were not in vain.

Further on down the dark pathway, we came to the point where we had turned around some months ago, from this point on we would be exploring unknown territory.

The trail was easy to hike except for the frequent large rocks we had to straddle. There was little change to our path for the next hour or so, only slightly varying left or right, and a slight drop in elevation.

We stopped to take a break in a fairly large room and while sitting there, we turned our lights off. We remained silent for the longest time—what seemed like an hour—just to listen for any sounds coming from the cavern up ahead of us. As we sat there in the total darkness, I noticed the bubbling and trickling sound of the stream seemed to be louder in the darkness. It's hard to imagine just how dark it is inside a cave (unless you've been spelunking). You can't close your eyes tight enough to block out all the light to compare it. I could hear what sounded like crickets or spring frogs just before dusk on an early summer afternoon, or so it seemed; it could have been just my imagination.

I imagine the stream must have been much larger when it began washing away the soil from this mountain, slowly enlarging the tunnel through hundreds or maybe even thousands of years of erosion (caused by the accumulation of snow, ice, and rain high up in the mountain's apex). It's hard to tell how far this cavern goes or where it may take us, but we are determined to find the source of the fresh air that fills the tunnel, and why the air is fresh.

The stream was getting deeper as we hiked further into the dark cavern, if we had a small boat or a canoe, we could float down the now small river.

We must have walked ten miles or more when we noticed what sounded like fast-moving water, maybe rapids or a waterfall I imagined. As we got closer, we found another stream coming from the wall on one side of the cavern merging to form a small river. A few hundred feet from where the waters merged, the (now single again) stream of water disappeared into the darkness. Moving in closer to get a better look at the vanishing waters exit point, I looked down to find a large pond being filled by a majestic waterfall. The sound of the water was amplified by the large circular empty cavern that was created by the flowing-water. The sound overtook our best attempts to communicate with each other.

Looking around, I was captivated by what appeared to be a naturally terraced stairway leading down each side of the waterfall, like a grand entranceway in an old southern mansion with the cascading waterfall as a brilliantly displayed centerpiece.

I motioned for Mike and Sid to follow me using my flashlight as a pointer. The steps looked natural at first glance then I noticed how evenly they were spaced, they were taller and wider than normal steps, yet all equally spaced, and after further inspection, I was convinced they were definitely not natural and most likely were carved by human hands.

The dark emerald pool at the bottom of the waterfall would measure at least thirty feet across and equally as long. Lined up around the pool of water were large oblong stones spaced about eight feet apart which appeared to be hand-carved. They were most likely seats for some kind of ancient ritual or maybe for worshiping some unknown gods. The whole place resembled some Incan alter from an old movie or a picture from a travel guide for Mexico. We found evenly spaced holes in the walls

around the pool, which were perhaps for holding torches or some primitive light source we imagined.

With the roaring of the falling water echoing through the cavern, our attempts to communicate with each other were hopeless. We had to move on downstream before we could even attempt to have a conversation. All along the sides of the stream, on the walls, were carvings and what looked like primitive drawings; strange bird-like creatures and lions or some kind of cats were in most of the drawings, while some child-like depictions of stick-people standing over a large buffalo or a mastodon served as the main feature of the ancient exhibit. Now it seemed, as though we may be on the verge of an important discovery.

We walked a good hundred yards away from the falls before we could understand each other, then we could discuss what we had just seen. We took pictures of everything then continued on our journey.

"How much further are we going, Dad?" Michael asked.

"That's up to you two. I hate to turn back now that we have finally found some signs of life," I admitted, "I don't believe this is your average tourist stop, do you?"

"I think we should keep going too, this may be the only chance we ever get to see who built this place," Sid added.

As we continued through the dark underworld, it became apparent to us that all the wonders we had seen were not the work of Mother Nature nor was it the work of anyone either of us had ever seen.

We came upon a burned-out campsite with trash strewn around, as if someone had just left from there. Bottles and cans dating back to the sixties lay in small piles (perhaps from a celebration some fifty years earlier) emptied and discarded for the scavengers to explore. Then we found more evidence of human existence like footprints in the dirt floor; they appeared to be normal sized human prints with five toes, probably belonging to a full-grown man.

"Let's be as quiet as we can, we don't want to run into a wild man," I warned.

We took another reading of the air before moving on, the needle on the meter didn't even move, the air was perfectly clean except for a trace of pollen.

We could hear the faint roar of the waterfall that we left behind some time ago along with the seldom rustle of denim rubbing together as we walked.

I noticed a familiar odor—the smell of flowering plants or trees as if it were springtime in a forest. I figured we must be near an opening in the cave. I could also hear the sound of water splashing like another waterfall, getting louder as we got closer.

I brushed aside what appeared to be honeysuckle vines and some species of ivy to reveal the cave opening that we had been seeking all this time. You could hardly make out where the cave ended and the forest began because of the thick vines and overgrowth encapsulating the entrance as if it were hiding some sort of a secret passage from the rest of the world.

There was little to no light to welcome us as we stepped out of the cave and into a strange but beautiful forest. Looking around, I noticed that the tops of the trees were so dense that they formed an almost waterproof canopy, blocking out the majority of the sunlight while leaving the underlying plants and vegetation to fight over the small rations of light to survive in a dark world. As I looked up to the apex of the forest, I witnessed the sun piercing through the jagged slender openings where two leaves had yet to meet, allowing tiny rays of light to escape giving the impression of a starry sky, while a few of the rays would reach the forest floor. Mushrooms and moss along with teaberry, mountain laurels, and ginseng seemed to be abundant in the sparse light, along with a few plants that I was not familiar with.

We must have traveled ten miles or more through the belly of the mountain to find this opening. We sat there quietly on a large flat rock overlooking one of the most beautiful forests you could imagine, just soaking up all the beauty of nature that we had been denied all these months while confined to our bland prison sanctuaries.

Why is this air fresh here yet on the other side of the mountain it's still toxic? That is something we needed to figure out before we left this place, I thought.

Now we needed to decide if we're going to keep going or declare this spot the end of our journey and go back to our shelters, never knowing who or what we may have discovered ahead.

"We should vote on this, it could change our lives," I said.

"Let's keep going for a few more hours, if we don't find anything unusual by noon we'll head back," Sid suggested.

"Michael, you have a say in this too, what do you say?"

"I'm for going on, we've come too far to stop now, we might be just a few feet away from a great discovery," he said.

"We've followed the stream this far, let's see where she takes us now."

The barely recognizable trail leading down the side of the falls was covered completely with entangled undergrowth, but we managed to make it to the forest floor where we found yet another spectacular vision from Mother Nature's scrapbook to delight our eyes. The cascading river was equally as grand as the first waterfall but cloaked in a fabulous green layer of vines with yellow and white wildflowers spread throughout like a handmade quilt displayed proudly on your grandmother's wall representing the grand entrance to the cavern.

The survival shows on television tell you to follow the rivers and streams if you want to find civilization, so we followed the stream through the forest where it led us to a run-down abandoned log cabin and two smaller sheds, probably for grain storage or livestock feed by the looks of them. The buildings appeared to be abandoned long ago, whoever lived there left some time ago.

We walked on following a small footpath that lead to a clearing which looked like it had been used recently. in the center of the clearing were the remnants of a fire. You could still smell the burnt wood as if someone had a bonfire there just a few days ago, and the smell of burnt pork lingered in the now cold ashes.

Still, further down the pathway, we discovered more cabins, and that's where we met Victor and Dolly. The couple looked middle-aged (thirty something), and in very good health. Their clothes were somewhat out of style for the year 2025 I noticed, more like the fashion of the sixties during the peace movement era. They welcomed us into their home and invited us to share a meal with them. We dined on some deliciously aged ham, fresh mushrooms, and ostrich-egg salad (which I found to be much better than my Grandma's recipe. Shh!).

We explained how we came through the cavern and how it leads to the other side of the mountain some twelve miles or more. Then they began to tell us their story.

Victor told us that his parents had come to the commune in the sixties at the height of the Vietnam War along with a couple dozen other freedom seekers all looking to escape the draft, and live and love in peace and tranquility. Victor was only eight years old at the time and Dolly wasn't even born yet. The freedom seekers lived there in peace and harmony and have been self-sufficient all these years, growing their own food and raising their livestock. They would take advantage of the medicinal properties of the local plants and herbs for their medical needs. All these years, they had only minor illnesses to confront. Rarely did anyone develop toothaches or colds or any of the usual ailments in society that they couldn't remedy with their herbs and the local water. No one ever had to leave the compound; everything they needed, they would make.

Victor's father (Charles Grant) who died just recently at the young age of ninety-four was the one that brought everyone to this site. Charles's father (Jacob Grant) was given a map to this place known through legends as 'the land where no-one ever grows old' when he was just a young man (in the late eighteen hundreds). Before Victor's grandfather died, he gave the map to his son (Charles). Victor's father would teach him everything he needed to know to survive in the wilderness.

When the draft lottery started in the sixties, Charles and his wife Theresa with their son led a group of rebels forty-three miles from the nearest sign of civilization through this still uncharted territory to this place they call Paradise. Legend has it that this was an Indian village once upon a time.

The water from the stream holds some kind of healing powers they told us, all the vegetables and plants thrived on the crystal-clear liquid. Rarely does anyone in their compound ever get sick and they credited this to the stream's water and the absence of preservatives from their naturally raised and grown foods, unlike the fast-foods (which most of us see as necessities in our society). All the vegetables they grew and the animals that they raised for food were nourished with the magical liquid, which only enhances the power of the nutrients that they get from the meat and the vegetables.

All the medicines they use are made with the water from the stream and they prepare all their meals using the same water too.

They told us of illnesses that were known to be incurable in our society, suddenly vanishing after being treated with this water. The miracle liquid would even reverse aging to a great extent. Just bathing or showering in the water had healing effects on skin disorders while removing stress and pains almost instantly.

"You mean like the fountain of youth?" I asked him.

"Yea, something like that," Victor replied.

They told us some original members of the community are over one hundred years old and they are still in very good shape. The emphasis on exercise was also a factor in their youthful longevity.

Victor told us that he was just a kid when they arrived at the camp in nineteen-sixty-five, maybe seven or eight years old at most, which would make him sixty-eight years old today. He doesn't look a day over thirty-five, and Dolly would be sixty but would pass for thirty.

Forty-three children had been born in the camp over the past sixty years, and just recently another fourth-generation baby was added to the group. All those children are still there, and they seem to be happy and healthy as can be.

The kids were full of questions about the outside world, so I told them that the reason we were here was because some people just can't get along with others, so they try to blow each other up.

At that moment, I knew we were sent there for some Divine reason and not just dumb luck. Something caused Michael's pick to make a hole through the wall and something caused the air to blow in his ear to get his attention. Our being here is no coincidence. Maybe we're here because of the water, I thought to myself.

Over the years, only a few of the members of the community ever chose to leave the compound, while swearing secrecy to the location and never to be seen again. Only two people have ever returned, and they regretted ever leaving their paradise. The outside world can seem cruel after you've lived here where everything is free, with no outside contact and no schedules, you might find it hard to give up. Just think, you never need money for anything, as long as everyone does their part to keep the animals fed and keep the gardens in good shape. There are no bills to pay, no taxes and no debts, which adds up to a Paradise in my book.

I asked Victor what he knew about the grand room with the stairway, the waterfall, and the old drawings on the walls. He said that the room is just as it was when they got there. They use it for special occasions and celebrations, like concerts and weddings. It seems the room has really good sound quality which makes for good concerts. They were taught to respect the place. Victor figures the place was made by the local Indians that once roamed the valley before migrating into the towns and cities a couple hundred years ago.

Victor and Dolly looked like they just stepped out of a Woodstock film, sixty years ago with their long hair, bell-bottoms, and tie-dyed t-shirts, right down to their peace sign tattoos and leather sandals.

They had lots of neighbors who lived in the nearby cabins. All were the original settlers or descendants of the original sixties'– rebels, all living a life of tranquility, without government regulations and taxes, or any sort of aid from the outside world, which left me feeling somewhat envious.

The group used a wind-up W.W.II CB radio to communicate with the outside world, while keeping their location secret, for over sixty years.

They raise their children to have respect and they teach them everything they need to know about life and surviving on their own without any help from the outside world.

They grow everything they need to eat; they even grow pot (for medicinal purposes as well as for pleasure). They grow cotton for bedding and clothing, and tobacco for smoking. They make their own wine, beer, and moonshine, as well as their own candles and soap from the livestock suet (fat) when they slaughter their animals. The forest supplies them with all the nuts and berries they want, as well as game to eat and all the lumber they need to build and heat their homes.

They had dogs and cats of several different mixed breeds as their loyal companions and best friends.

They had no computers, no cell phones or televisions nor did they have mail service to distract them from their daily lives. They had only frequent reminders of the outside world; some old silverware, pots and pans, an ivory comb, and a handful of books (that had been recovered several times). Everything had been handed down for three generations and treasured as if they were sacred heirlooms. Small things that we wouldn't give a second thought to, were treasures to them. There was a sense of innocence all around; it was as if we stepped into a time warp, where time had remained unchanged for sixty-some years.

For entertainment, they had concerts: some people playing guitars, harmonicas, and tambourines. All holding on to the traditions of their rebel predecessors, memorizing the sixties songs as if they were their Declaration of Independence or National Anthem, that was the last music they heard from the outside world. They would have talent contests allowing the children to perform songs or tell stories around a bonfire, enjoying life and celebrating freedom; no entry fees or concession costs, everything is always free, self-sufficient living to be envied.

When the members of the community heard of a nuclear missile launch (which was much later than our last report), they used the cave for protection from the fallout. Victor said that the point of contact for the missile was just off the west coast, not the east as we thought it would be. That might explain the toxic air on the other side of the mountain (where our caves are), Sid explained. The dense forest canopy that blocks out most of the sun, would shield them from most of the toxins while the heavy rains washed away what remained of the poison.

Their knowledge of the plants and herbs and the medicinal values of each species helped them to care for almost any ailment, which enabled them to survive without modern medicines.

We told them about the caves (we had been stuck in) since the nuclear attack, and how we just happened upon the entranceway that would lead us to their hidden paradise.

I showed Victor and Dolly my smartphone and explained to them all the things you could do with it (when you have a good reception that is). They were amazed by modern technology but could see no reason to have the device in their world. Dolly, along with most of the younger people, who had gathered around to hear us talk about the outside world, had never even seen a phone, along with many other modern devices developed since 1965.

The sun was going down on our little get-together and we were getting ready to leave when Victor asked us to stay the night. He said we could get an early start in the morning after we've had a good breakfast. As for me, I was exhausted and I thought Sid and Mike could use some sleep too. We agreed unanimously to stay the night. We had a great time, talking about the problems going on in the world (that they choose to live without)–the good things as well as the bad.

To watch Victor and Dolly interact with each other, both so laid-back and carefree and still in love, you have to envy their lifestyle. It's like something that's been missing from our world for a long time now (simple human affection) where no one has time for relaxing and holding hands with each other. The simple act of cuddling together is rarely seen in today's world. All the children we met were polite and eager to hear our tales of modern life of which they knew nothing about. Someday, they may want to leave their simple world to explore the great outdoors, they should at least have their own choice. If it were me, I would most likely stay here.

Our beds were handmade from materials that were grown in their village; feather-tick mattresses (made with their cotton and stuffed with feathers from their geese) on wooden frames (from the forest and willow-bark straps for springs). They had handmade patchwork quilts with feed–sacks backing (with the pictures of a pig or cow still on them). I was taken back to my grandfather's farm in Virginia when I was just a boy, I can't recall sleeping any better. Dolly has everything here to make a good breakfast (that we would have at home): bacon, eggs, biscuits, and her own special blueberry jam, and the coffee they grow is better than my favorite brand.

Victor gave us a few things to take back with us: some bacon, eggs, jam, and coffee, and a bag of stone-ground flour that Dolly prepared herself.

To keep this place secret all these years without any government interference and to raise their children without all the modern technologies (that our kids see as necessities), seems almost impossible to me. It's like a dream that I use to have and thought was gone long ago, yet here it is staring me in the face. I asked Victor if we would be welcomed if we wanted to join their happy community. He replied that as long as we promise to keep this place a secret and we do our part for the community, we were welcome to come and go as we please, just try not to disrupt their serenity.

Enough dreaming, we had to be getting back to our families, they were probably worried sick. But before we went, I just wanted to let Victor know that if they ever want to get to the big city, they should just follow the stream, and be sure to lock the door behind them. I gave him a key to the front door of the cave before we left.

We said one more goodbye to our new friends before we began our trip back through the mountain. With a new feeling of accomplishment, I could not have been more satisfied with our findings if I had found King Tuts tomb.

I was so relieved for my parents back in Virginia, after hearing the news from Victor. Who would have thought that the west coast would be the target for Iran's missile attack instead of Washington, D.C.

The first thing we did when we got back to our families was to construct a door for the cavern entrance, knowing that wild animals could easily wander into our homes from the forest (if they want to walk twelve miles for a meal).

In the days following our trip through the mountain passage, I couldn't help but dream of the life the young rebels that started the compound must have enjoyed. Living off the land, neighbor helping neighbor, building what they needed to survive and planting and raising what they needed to eat, not worrying about how much this cost's or how much they got paid or how much tax they owed. I was undoubtedly meant to live in an earlier century. It's not every day the taste of freedom knocks at your door inviting you to partake in its wondrous bounty. I can't seem to get it off my mind, every night the dream comes back, it's almost like someone or something was trying to tell me 'this is where you belong', all you have to do is reach out and take it.

Two weeks have passed since we visited our secretive friends (where we stood in the clean, fresh air). The air outside our safe house is still too toxic for us to leave our confines.

I believe with a little luck, I could convince Laura and the kids to make the long trek through the cavern, to see the place I call Paradise and to get outside in the fresh air. After all, the girls have been stuck inside for almost a year now. They would love to get out of this cave.

We decided to recalibrate the air test meters to be sure that they were working. After all, we had good readings on the other side of the mountain while here, at our cave, the air is still toxic.

After another week of disappointing readings of the air quality, we voted unanimously to pay a visit to our hippie friends on the other side of the mountain, for the fresh air if nothing else.

We didn't know how long we would be staying at the commune so we took only enough food to last a couple of days (which was most of our remaining food supply), some pots and pans and silverware (that I figured Dolly could use).

The lack of physical activity was painfully evident as we slowly made our way down the dark tunnel. You don't realize how out of shape you are until you try to use your pampered muscles a little more than usual, and I know one girl that's going to be sore tomorrow. We had to stop and rest several times and we spent a couple hours looking at the scenery and taking pictures of the falls and wall carvings, but we made it to the resort in just over twelve hours, recovery time would surpass that.

Laura could not believe how beautiful the hidden paradise was, and she felt the same way that I did about living there. If we didn't have three kids to think about and we could go back about twenty years, we most likely would stay here.

You would think we gave Dolly a million dollars when she saw the pots and pans that we brought her; she had been using worn-out cookware that had been handed down for seventy-five years.

We've been here three days now and everyone is getting used to the care-free lifestyle, not to mention the clean fresh air.

The kids have made lots of new friends here while learning to live without the electronic games and television shows, learning to eat good nutritious food and getting plenty of exercise with their new friends.

We have been shut off from our normal everyday lives on the outside for almost a year now, we don't even know if our friends are still there, or if we still have our jobs and homes to go back to. We need to try to contact Mom and Dad; they probably gave us up for dead after all this time.

Victor's radio did pick up some static from a couple of truckers, and we were able to relay a message to my brother's neighbor Fat-Back (a long-haul trucker we have known for years), and he promised to get hold of Steve today with a message: everyone's fine.

As good as it sounds to stay here, we have to think of the kids and what is best for them. We're not yet ready to give up our hospitals and shopping malls, not with young children still to raise, we can always come back to visit.

I discussed the healing powers of the water with Victor and Sid and thought it best to let them decide whether we should introduce the water to the world so it can benefit everyone or to keep it secret. If we could just find a way to access the water without jeopardizing the location of Paradise, everyone would be happy.

Victor mentioned that the river's path doesn't stop in Paradise but keeps going for many miles before it joins Bear Creek, he said the stream even disappears underground then comes back out a few miles further down the mountain.

"That's it!" I said, "We'll go down the mountain to where the stream comes back out of the ground and use that for the source, that way we won't lead anybody here."

"Hopefully, the water still has its healing powers downstream," Sid mentioned.

"I'll take you two down tomorrow and show you the spot where the water comes out of the ground, maybe you can test it to see."

Victor had three horses saddled and ready to go the next morning, about three hours down and three back he said. I was raised on horseback, but I think Sid was having a little trouble controlling his mount. Thankfully, we made the trip without any major problems.

The stream disappeared into the ground at least a mile back from where it comes back out of the ground, which should keep Paradise a secret, we figured.

The next day we would leave Paradise on horse-back, traveling the same trail that the freedom seekers used some sixty years ago. They were seeking freedom from war. As for us, I think we found freedom in Paradise.

It's good to know that we can go back to the hidden paradise, to the world that time forgot, whenever we need to take a break from the digital, artificial, computerized fast-paced world that we live in today.

America's missile defense system was used to destroy Iran's missiles before they could reach our shores and cause too much damage, but the fallout from the blast would linger over the western states for years to come; the clean-up continues today.

Only a handful of people were contaminated, though many were affected by the fall-out. The soil would be contaminated as well as the vegetation and crops in a five-hundred-mile radius of the blast.

The U.S. retaliated against Iran by destroying all their nuclear storage facilities as well as missile factories above and below ground. All the world leaders have agreed not to sell any weapons of any kind to Iran in the future.

As for the Osgoods, we are getting back to our lives. While things have changed since the attack, we still have our home, our family and friends, and I still have my job; making it easier for doctors to save lives.

We're going to Bristol this weekend to see Mom and Dad. It's been a long time since I had a good hug, and sat down to eat Sunday dinner together. Remember: you have to make time to be together in this fast-moving world. One day you'll turn around and it will all be gone.

We go to see Victor and Dolly every year now. Laura and I would stay there if we didn't have kids, maybe when they're all grown up and on their own, we'll retire there, in Paradise.

The Bear Creek water co. was built on the site where the water came out of the ground. Tests have shown the water does have some healing effects, though not the same as the water in Paradise, but it's being used in bottled water and some medicines now.

www.ingramcontent.com/pod-product-compliance
Lightning Source LLC
LaVergne TN
LVHW041551060526
838200LV00037B/1235